PUFFIN BOOKS

Stinkers Ahoy!

Roger McGough was born in Liverpool and in the late sixties and early seventies he was a member of the group The Scaffold. Author of over thirty books for both children and adults, Roger McGough has done much to popularize poetry. A frequent broadcaster and an occasional playwright, he now lives in London.

Other books by Roger McGough

Poetry

HELEN HIGHWATER
AN IMAGINARY MENAGERIE
LUCKY: A BOOK OF POEMS
MY DAD'S A FIRE-EATER
NAILING THE SHADOW
PILLOW TALK
SKY IN THE PIE
YOU TELL ME (*with Michael Rosen*)

PUFFIN PORTABLE POETS (*with Brian Patten and Kit Wright*)

Poetry for older readers

STRICTLY PRIVATE (*Ed.*)
YOU AT THE BACK

Fiction

THE GREAT SMILE ROBBERY
THE STOWAWAYS

Roger McGough

Stinkers Ahoy!

Illustrated by Tony Blundell

PUFFIN BOOKS

PUFFIN BOOKS

Published by the Penguin Group
Penguin Books Ltd, 27 Wrights Lane, London W8 5TZ, England
Penguin Books USA Inc., 375 Hudson Street, New York, New York 10014, USA
Penguin Books Australia Ltd, Ringwood, Victoria, Australia
Penguin Books Canada Ltd, 10 Alcorn Avenue, Toronto, Ontario, Canada M4V 3B2
Penguin Books (NZ) Ltd, 182–190 Wairau Road, Auckland 10, New Zealand

Penguin Books Ltd, Registered Offices: Harmondsworth, Middlesex, England

First published by Viking 1995
Published in Puffin Books 1996
1 3 5 7 9 10 8 6 4 2

Text copyright © Roger McGough, 1995
Illustrations copyright © Tony Blundell, 1995
All rights reserved

The moral right of the author and illustrator has been asserted

Filmset in Sabon

Made and printed in England by Clays Ltd, St Ives plc

1.

Chapter One

2 Cargoes

If you are wondering what happened to Chapter One,
I'll tell you. It has sunk without trace.
It was raided, boarded, plundered and set fire to,
by that most wicked of pirates, Two-eyed Jack,
the curse of the Spanish Main.

Nothing was sacred, nobody was safe, when Jack
Masefield and his beastly one-eyed crew set sail
aboard the *Sea Fever*, the Jolly Roger fluttering
astern like a mad dog's snarl.

Stately Spanish galleons,
laden with doubloons,
balloons, tiaras, tortillas
and crystal flagons of
rare medicines for
the royal coughers,
were ransacked
and
sent
spinning
to
the
bottom
of
the
ocean.

Quinqueremes, bound for sunny Palestine with cargoes of old spices, aftershave, silks and silly sandals, were looted and booted into kingdom come.

Even dirty British coasters, their smoke-stacks coated with salt, were trampled on and discarded like cheap tin trays.

But, as in all good adventure films, the baddies were finally caught and brought to justice.

And as Two-eyed Jack and his crew were captured, found guilty and sentenced to eighteen months' community service, the whole cinema audience cheered and applauded.

(The whole cinema audience, that is, except for the Stinkers.)

The Stinkers, who booed and booed and boooooed.

3 Mug Shots

If you have read *The Great Smile Robbery*, you can skip this chapter. If not, let me give you a low-down on the Stinkers. And I mean,   down:

low

Billy Bogie —

A nose-picker of great renown
Who leaves his mark all over town.

King Pong –

The concrete jungle is his domain
Keep well clear (he smells like a drain).

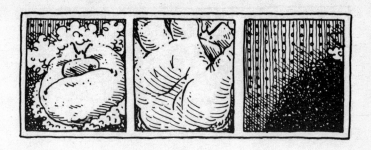

Mrs Wobblebottom –

The only lady in the pack
Give her a buffalo pasty, you'll not get it back.

Old Sourpuss –

A mangier cat you're unlikely to meet
To avoid him, fleas cross over the street.

Nick O'Teen –

Smoking is his passion
Lungs like prunes, his face is ashen.

Now that you have met them, do you still want to
carry on with the story?

OK. But you have been warned!

4 Mayhem

'I wish I could be a black-hearted
villain like Two-eyed Jack,'
sighed Nick O'Teen, as the gang
trundled down the high street in search of a burger.

'You probably are,' said King Pong, 'with all that
tar and gunge inside you.'

Nick O'Teen coughed indignantly.

Their search ended when Mrs W.B. spotted
a burger. It was on top of a litter-bin
outside McDougall's.

'I saw it first,' she screamed, breaking
into a gallop.

Window-gazers, arm-in-armers
and big-spenders were elbowed aside
as the Stinkers charged along the pavement
like a pack of Rugby League forwards with their
shorts on fire.

Mrs W.B. got there first, but only just. No sooner had she freed the half-eaten burger from the garbage when King Pong leaped upon her back and brought her to the ground.

Billy Bogie dived into the scrum, followed by Sourpuss and a panting Nick O'Teen.

It was Mayhem.

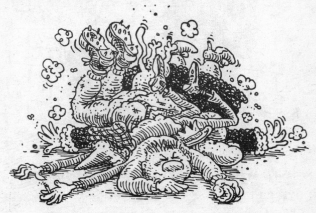

'Look out, it's Mayhem,' said Billy, through a mouthful of congealed beef.

'Inspector Mayhem to you,' said the Inspector, a
tall lantern-jawed man with a seven o'clock shadow,
known around Scotland Yard as The Blue Lamp.
'And what do you think you're a doing of?'

The gang scrambled to its feet.

'Er . . . we . . . . .   .   ∞   we . . . were . . .'
'Er . . . er . . . .'
'We were . . .   . er . . .'

'Practising making a citizen's arrest,' said King Pong, fibber-in-chief.

'What's a citizen's arrest?' whispered Sourpuss.

'It means taking the law into your own hands,' explained Mrs Wobblebottom.

'But I don't have any hands,' said Sourpuss, and then squealed as she handbagged him on the nose.

'Mm, a likely story,' said the Inspector. 'Just be very careful in future, that's all. You Stinkers are well known down at the police-station, and if there's a hint of any more trouble I shall have to put a tail on you.'

'But I've already got a tail on me,' said Sourpuss, and then squealed as Mrs W.B. handbagged him on the nose. Again.

5 Down in the Frown

That same evening (or, it might have been the
following Wednesday) the Stinkers sat gloomily in
the back room of the Frown and Misery.

'It's boring round here,' said Billy, 'dead boring.'
And removing a finger from a cavern deep in his left
nostril, said dreamily, 'Pot-holing sounds good. Why
don't we go to the Peak District and do that?'

'Some of us seem able to do it right here,'
remarked Mrs W.B. rather pointedly.

'Oh, very funny,' sniffed Billy.

'Billy's right, though,' said Nick O'Teen, 'about
being boring. As that Inspector Mayhem said, we are
so well known around here we can't do a naughty
thing without the police jumping on us. It's a
bloomin' liberty.'

Everyone agreed it was a bloomin' liberty.

. . . .
. . . Nobody said a word for 28.7 seconds exactly, and then King Pong said, 'Switch on the telly, there might be something to cheer us up, like a storm in a tea-cup or a plague of cockroaches.'

The Stinkers warmed to the possibilities.

'Perhaps an oil-tanker's run aground and there's an oil slick on the beach at Blackpool . . .'

'But the holiday-makers don't notice.'

'Perhaps there's a documentary about the sticky bits of fluff you find down the back of the sofa.'

'Or a food programme showing you how to make kipper and custard quiche . . .'

. . . 'And home-brewed cod-liver-oil wine.'

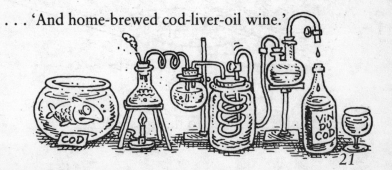

They settled now in eager anticipation as the TV set crackled into life.

As soon as they recognized the programme, they howled with disappointment and buried their heads in their hands (although, in Billy's case, it was vice versa).

It was the weekly *Smile* programme hosted by Emerson, the most popular TV personality in the whole world.

6 Emerson

If you have read *The Great Smile Robbery*, or intend to one day, then you can skip this chapter.

Emerson used to live down the road from the Stinkers. In fact, he still has a house there, but now spends most of his time jetting around the world helping to make people smile and be happy.

The Stinkers couldn't stand him when he was a cheerful nobody, but when he won a smile competition and went on television, and someone wrote a book about him, the Stinkers loathed him more than anything.

More than toothpaste, even.

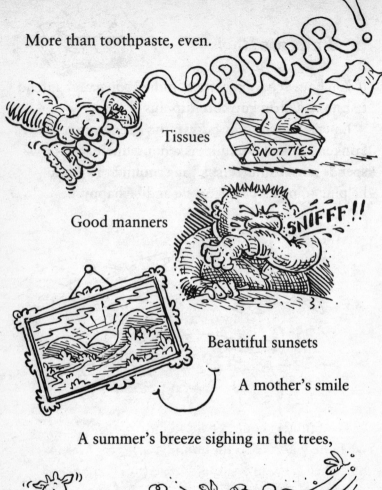

Tissues

SNOTTIES

Good manners

SNIFFF!!

Beautiful sunsets

A mother's smile

A summer's breeze sighing in the trees,

etc., etc.

Bambi, _____ etc., etc., etc.

7 Welcome Back

Nothing much has happened in the Frown and Misery while you have been away.

The television set, of course, has been switched off. The chairs and tables picked up, the broken glasses cleared and the ashtrays emptied (by Nick O'Teen, who enjoys a mouthful between smokes).

But the atmosphere is very heavy indeed. In fact, it is so heavy that the ceiling bends under its weight and the walls buckle. If you were to enter that room now you would have to go in on all fours.

Suddenly, King Pong had the germ of an idea. He examined it closely before crushing it between finger and thumb.

'Pirates,' he said. 'Pirates.'

As the others looked at him, with growing interest, the room resumed its normal size.

'Let's sail away from here and become pirates!'

There was a pause . . . .
. . . . (5.08 secs) and then everybody
began talking at once.

The pirate queen of the Barbary Coast, freebooting in kneeboots and eating the most!

Unscrambled, this is what they said:

Mrs W.B.: 'The pirate queen of the Barbary Coast,
freebooting in kneeboots and eating the most!'

B.B.: 'Billy Bogie, the bold buccaneer,
with a ring through his nose instead of his ear!'

O.S.: 'Old Sourpuss, the scourge of the seven seas,
with three wooden legs attached to his knees!'

'And the great thing,' added Nick O'Teen,
'is that we'd be oceans away from Inspector Mayhem
and his spoilsport policemen.'

'We could rob, pillage and plunder to our heart's
content,' sighed Billy dreamily.

'Kidnap Emerson,' said Mrs W.B., 'and make him
walk the plank.'

Everybody guffawed and chortled wildly.

King Pong put up a hand solemnly and said,
'But to do that we'd need a plank.'

The others nodded and gave the matter some
thought.

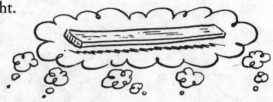

King Pong continued, 'And not only a plank,
but a ship to put under it.'

'That could be the difficult part,' admitted Billy.

The only sound that then there was,
was the thound of thinkers stinking.

I'm sorry. I mean, the sound of stinkers thinking.

8   *Going to the Fayre*

Outskirts Park is on the outskirts of town, and every year the Summer Fayre is held there. Local craftsfolk set up their stalls. There are coconut shies and pony-rides; Punch and Judy and fancy dress competitions; a fun-fair, refreshments, and music provided by the local hospital radio.

It was a glorious day and everybody was in fine fettle.

Five, however, were in foul fettle. The Stinkers schlepped their way through the crowds, grabbing handfuls of candy-floss from passing toddlers. Always on the look out for a dropped coin,

a discarded sandwich,

a squeezable carton.

It had been Mrs W.B.'s idea to come to the Fayre. 'It will take our minds off things,' she reasoned, 'and besides, I want to have a go on the Bouncy Castle.'

The trouble was (and this explains their foul mood), the trouble was, that the man in charge of the Bouncy Castle wouldn't let Mrs Wobblebottom near it.

'Children only,' he said, 'elephants, hippopotamuses and ladies over two tonnes not permitted.'

Mrs W.B. was furious. So much so, that she snatched a raspberry ripple from a little girl in a pretty pink dress who had been waiting patiently in a long queue outside the ice-cream van for all of twenty minutes.

'You've not heard the end of this,' she shouted, and would have shouted more had the voice on the loudspeaker not interrupted.

'Hurry on over to the stage area, folks, where the singing competition is about to begin. Cash prizes for the winners! Let's have some more volunteers. Roll up! Roll up!'

While Nick O'Teen rolled up, King Pong became excited. 'I can sing,' he said, 'I can sing.'

The others looked dubious.

'I can when there's money to be won, and you can all help by cheering me and booing everybody else. Let's go.'

9 The King Lives

The first entrant thought he was Paul McCartney.

Unfortunately nobody else did, because he looked like Quasimodo and sounded like Popeye.

A pair of identical twins came next. One sang an aria from *Madame Butterfly* and the other 'Puff, the Magic Dragon' (at the same time). The audience found it all very confusing.

The third entrant was the little girl in the pretty pink dress. She sang the first verse of 'Somewhere over the Rainbow' quite beautifully, and then, spotting Mrs Wobblebottom in the audience, burst into tears and fled sobbing into the far, far distance.

King Pong, hearing the knock of opportunity, clambered on to the stage and seized the microphone. In what he fondly imagined was an American deep-Southern drawl, he introduced himself: 'The King lives, guys and gals, and I'm gonna sing for you here right now a little number I wrote with an old buddy of mine, B.J. Bogie, and it goes something like this right here . . . It's called "Don't be My Teddy Bear".'

When it's picnic-time for teddy bears
To the woods without delay
We eat their cakes and drink their juice
And chase those bears away.

'Cos we're the famous Stinkers
We love to make a noise
What we hate are teddy bears
And little cuddly toys.

We're the lowest of the low
Cause Bruin ruin wherever we go
From Liverpool to Luton, Beds.,
We play soccer with teddy bears' 'eads.

'Cos we're the famous Stinkers
We love to make a noise
What we hate are teddy bears
And little cuddly toys.

(So if you've got a teddy bear in your home
Better watch out when you're alone
'Cos one dark night we'll make a call
Bash that teddy – you and all!)

38

'Cos we're the famous Stinkers
We love to make a noise
And what we hate the very most
Are cuddly girls and boys.

As King Pong sang, eyes closed, belting out chords on an imaginary guitar, he was unaware of the audience dwindling in droves. Concerned parents shooed away their children. Dear old ladies turned off their hearing-aids and headed for the tea tent. Even a bevvy of lager louts blushed and hung their shaven heads in shame.

By the time he had finished (and only
then did the birds return to the trees)
the DJ and organizers of the competition were loading
their equipment into the back of their van.

'Where's my prize money, then?' demanded Pong.

'Aye, he put Pavarotti to shame,' said Mrs
Wobblebottom, 'not to mention Caruso.'*

'Elton John, eat your heart out,' said Billy B.

Without a word, the radio crew climbed aboard,
banged shut the doors and raced back to the local
hospital for some local anaesthetic and a lie-down.

---

* Robinson Caruso, a famous opera singer who lived on a
desert island.

10 A Fire-engine

At many an outdoor gathering one of the main
attractions is the fire-engine. Often there is a
breath-taking display by the local fire-brigade, and
afterwards children are allowed to climb aboard the
engine, and the lucky ones sit behind the steering
wheel and imagine they are driving across town at
breakneck speed, sirens screeching.

The Summer Fayre in Outskirts Park was no
exception, and as the Stinkers slouched past, the last
of the children was being helped down before the
firemen broke for a cup of tea and a bun.

'Stupid firemen,' muttered Billy B.

'Yes, interfering old busybodies,' agreed Nick.

'Just when the house has caught nicely alight, and before the blaze really gets going, down the street they come, making a huge racket, and put it out. A waste of time if you ask me.'

'They should leave well alone,' agreed Nick O'Teen. 'I like a nice inferno myself.'

'Oh, I think they're wonderful,' sighed Sourpuss, who had a soft spot for firemen ever since one had rescued him from a tree when he was a kitten.

'Firemen are my favourites,' he mused, and then added, 'next to sardines.'

A sudden ear-piercing screech startled everybody.

At first they thought it was the siren, but then realized it was Mrs W.B., who was jumping up and down in a state of high excitement.

'The Bouncy Castle,' she shrieked between jumps. 'I know how I can get into it.'

King Pong tutted. 'No, the man who owns the castle, the Duke, or whoever he is, he'll never let you in.'

Mrs W.B. stopped jumping (and the grass all around let out a deep sigh of relief).

'But he won't see me because I'm not going in through the entrance.'

'Then how are you going in?' asked Pong.

Mrs Wobblebottom turned and pointed at the fire-engine.

a stunned silence

a stunned silence

a stunned silence

There was a stunned silence which would have gone on for page after page had Billy not said,

'You mean, you're going to steal the fire-engine and ram-raid the castle? Yippee!'

'Gggrrreat!' said Sourpuss.

'No, no, no, no,' said Mrs W.B. 'What we're going to do is . . . push the fire-engine into that wood over there.' She pointed to a clump of trees directly behind the Bouncy Castle. 'I climb on to the ladder, we aim it in the direction of the castle, someone presses the button, and up I go.'

'Good golly, Mrs Wobblebottom,' gasped King Pong, his eyes shining with admiration. 'You mean, you're going to . . . you're actually going to . . .'

45

Mrs W.B. nodded. 'Yes, when I'm high above the Bouncy Castle . . . I jump!'

'Sensational!' said Nick O'Teen.

'Spectacular!' said Sourpuss.

'Megastinko!' said Billy.

'My hero!' said King Pong and kissed her full on the cheek.

Mrs Wobblebottom blushed and blushed until her face was as red as . . .

(see chapter heading)

11 Stairway to Paradise

After much huffing and puffing, the Stinkers managed to push the fire-engine into the wooded area, where it was hidden from view.

Knowing that they were taking part in one of the most daredevilish feats of all time, the Stinkers set about their tasks like a highly disciplined team. (All except Sourpuss, that is, who climbed up into the nearest tree and pretended to be stuck, in the hope that a handsome fireman might come to the rescue.)

Soon the turntable was in position and the ladder pointing in the direction of the Bouncy Castle.

Somewhere in the distance a brass band began playing as Mrs Wobblebottom, with a final wave to the Stinkers, climbed up the ladder. When she was on the top rung and holding tight, King Pong pressed the button. The music swelled and the clouds seemed to roll back as the ladder extended up, up into the sky. It seemed she would go on for ever,
Mrs Wobblebottom transformed into a queen, radiant and majestic, surrounded by a halo of golden sunbeams, ascending into heaven.

With a sudden jolt the ladder locked into place.
Below, the Stinkers held their breath as their heroine,
holding the top rung firmly with both hands, swung
herself out and over, to dangle perilously hundreds
of feet above the ground.

The music stopped. And as if on cue,
Mrs Wobblebottom dropped like a stone.

12 Crash-landing

On the floor of the Bouncy Castle children were . . .
(yes, you've guessed) bouncing.

up   up   up   up

and   and   and and   and   and

down   down   down

. . . and having a right good bouncy time.

Then, one by one, they became aware of a dark
shadow growing bigger and bigger.

A whistling sound, a rush of air.

They looked up . . . and screamed!

Was it a jumbo jet crash-landing!

A whale in search of an ocean?

A dinosaur dropping through the mists of time?

They didn't stop to think but leaped off
in all directions.
And not a moment too soon.

13 Unlucky for Some

The Big Bang was heard all over the county.
Some people thought it was an earthquake;
others, that a fireworks factory had exploded. Very few
recognized the sound of a Bouncy Castle bursting.

Marquees and amusement arcades were blown
over. The carousel went spinning over the trees like a
giant frisbee, and the Big Wheel rolled
out of the park and down the
road for several miles.

The owner of the Bouncy Castle (or, rather, the owner of several hundred pieces of coloured plastic) was furious. But he was also unconscious, having been catapulted, head first, into the Punch and Judy booth.

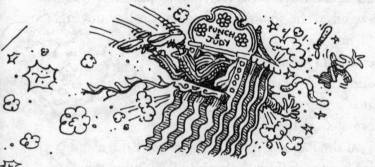

The Stinkers, led by King Pong, were soon upon the scene. They helped Mrs Wobblebottom out of the crater and, hardly able to walk for giggling, led her away, before the police, firemen, St John Ambulance Brigade, Boy Scouts, Girl Guides and other busybodies arrived.

14 Bloodcurdling Adventures

On the far side of the park was a large boating lake and it was towards this that the Stinkers were headed, although only Mrs Wobblebottom knew why.

'When I was on top of the ladder,' she explained, 'I could see for miles around, and I spotted something that is going to make our stinkiest dreams come true.'

Past the Pagoda, over the Japanese Bridge and there it was, anchored off a small island in the middle of the lake – a pirate ship!

The Stinkers stopped in their tracks.

'Meeow!' gasped Sourpuss.

'You said it,' chorused Billy, who was beside himself with excitement.

'Let's nick a couple of rowing boats, sail over there, sneak up on the crew, duff them up and feed 'em to the sharks.'

'One thing at a time,' said King Pong, putting the two Billys back together.

'Anyway, they're not real pirates, they're dummies dressed up.'

And so they were. The Pirate Ship, the Japanese Garden, the Dutch Windmill and the Indian Reservation (two tents and a plastic totem-pole) were all that remained of the International Garden Festival held some years before, when dozens of people from all over the neighbourhood had flocked to it and yawned.

'Snifferoody,' said Billy, 'then it's ours for the taking.'

''Ang on, 'ang on,' said Mrs W.B., 'there are some pretty angry firemen on our trail.'

'Not to mention the Bouncy Castle man,' mentioned Nick.

'Hexactly, so I suggest we find somewhere to hide until it gets dark, then, when everybody has gone home, we climb aboard, set sail for foreign parts and have bloodcurdling adventures.'

'Yeh!' said Billy, said King Pong, said Sourpuss, said Nick O'Teen.

'Yeh! Bloodcurdling adventures.'

'Bloodcurdling adventures,' echoed a parrot, perched high up in a tree.

15 Question and Answer

In a secluded corner of the park sits a nice clean shed where the gardeners get changed, wash and have their tea-breaks. (Although they are not at work today, there is tea, fresh milk in the fridge and biscuits in the tin.) Behind it, between the compost heap and the doggy toilet, is a shabby little greenhouse where the park-keeper goes to skive when there is work to be done.

Question: If you had the choice, where would you hide?

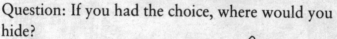

(a) The nice clean shed? Very good. This means that you are highly intelligent and good at hiding.

(b) The shabby little greenhouse? This means that you are either a Stinker, or a close relative and need a good hiding.

What attracted the Stinkers to the greenhouse was
the smell of manure, the dust and the cobwebs. They
are all crowded in now, munching slugs and taking it
in turn to breathe.

'It's hot and stuffy in here,' said Nick O'Teen,
lighting up a cigarette.

'Soon fix that,' said Billy and, picking up a stone, threw it at one of the glass panes, which shattered in amazement.

'Good fun, eh?' said Billy, reaching for another stone.

'People in glass houses shouldn't throw stones,' said Mrs Wobblebottom.

'Why not?' asked Billy and threw another.

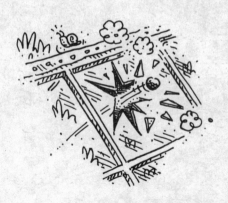

16 Why People in Glass Houses Shouldn't Throw Stones

The sound of breaking glass could be heard all over the park.

17 The Greenhouse Effect

In the boiling heat of the late afternoon the Stinkers
sweat, pick, scratch, squeeze, belch and
watch the leaves curl up in disgust.

They say rude things, and when the tomatoes
blush, eat them.

It is not a pretty sight so let us hurry away.

18 Jolly Roger's Sisters

Although most pirates were undoubtedly men, some of the fiercest have been women, who, for domestic reasons, worked only part time and so have been unjustly neglected by historians.

Agatha Tittletat, for instance, who during the week was manageress of a tea shop in Cheltenham, but at weekends became 'Black Aggie', the beast of the Bay of Biscay.

Noted for her wacky sense of humour, she would blindfold her enemies and make them walk the plank (when the ship was tied up at the quayside).

Captain Ivy Benson and her all-girl band of buxom buccaneers, whose deadly musical instruments caused havoc in naval garrisons all over the Mediterranean.

Captain Falsebeard, infamous for drinking rum and using foul language, was, in real life, Henrietta Rhodes-Royce, who, in the privacy of her own cabin, knitted peg-leg covers, embroidered nice Jolly Roger flags, and drank only cocoa (as well as the occasional glass of lager).

Not to be confused with *Captain Realbeard* (Mary 'Hairy' Carey), who chewed lead instead of bubblegum and blew cannonballs. A giant of a woman, her bite was worse than her barque. Every inch a feminist, they say her ghost still sails the seven seas in search of men who make jokes about lady pirates.

At nine o'clock the Stinkers were awakened from dreams of treasure islands and dead men's chests filled with gold, cheeseburgers and deep-fried pizzas by the sudden clang of park gates being banged shut.

This was the signal they had been waiting for!

One by one they emerged from what remained of the greenhouse, made straight for the jetty, climbed into a boat, and, by the light of the silvery moon, rowed across the lake to the pirate ship.

Imagine the excitement they felt! A new life filled with adventure beckoned.

No more trudging the streets in search of an empty corner to hang around.

No more begging from buskers.

No more rummaging through the litter-bin of life.

Of course, a few minor details had yet to be worked out. Like how to get the ship out of the lake, over the railings, along the street, down the motorway and into the sea. But that was a hurdle they would clear when they came to it.

And as they rowed, they all began to sing, ever so softly, the Stinkers' Boating Song:

> If you steal sweets from babies
> And push to the front of the queue
> If you hate soap and water
> Then we're the gang for you.
> *Row, boys, Row!*
>
> If you cheer on the baddies
> See the goodies and shout 'Boo!'
> If you're a secret stinker
> Then we're the gang for you.
> *Haul away, Haul away!*
>
> If you like smelling armpits
> Doggy breath and camel poo
> If teacher's always on your back
> Then we're the gang for you.
> *Blow, me bully boys, Blow!*

Yes, there was magic in the air!

20 Over the Top?

Getting the ship out of the lake, over the
railings, along the street, down the
motorway and into the sea, turned out,
in fact, to be a hurdle they neither cleared
nor came to.

Once the rowing boat was alongside,
Mrs Wobblebottom, moving with the speed
of a woman twice her size, elbowed the others out of
the way and was first over the handrail.

Once on deck, they all paused for a moment to get their breaths back and to take in the beauty of the scene:

The steady rocking of the ship; the creak of the anchor; the idle flapping of the sails in the breeze; the gentle lapping of the waves below; and above, the moon, its sister ship, about to set sail and guide them across the starry ocean.

'Enough of this rubbish,' said Pong, 'let's strip those dummies and dress up as pirates.'
'Yeh,' cried the Stinkers.

21 Surprise, Surprise

'GGGRRRRRR...' screamed the dummies.

The Stinkers froze in horror as the dummy pirates suddenly came to life and charged at them from all directions.

Down the mast, up the stairs, through the portholes, out of the woodwork they came, a screaming, terrifying horde of fierce buccaneers.

Before you could say:
CRICKERLANGERMANGERDOODLEDOO
the Stinkers were overpowered and roped together
around the foot of the mast.

Nick O'Teen, his voice shaking with fear,
whispered, 'Mrs Wobblebottom, if they make us
walk the plank, will you go first?'

'Why?' asked Mrs Wobblebottom.

'Because I can't swim, so if you jumped in first you
would splash all the water out of the lake.'

Mrs W.B. was about to reply with the full force of
her handbag when the Chief Pirate stepped forward.
'That's enough of that,' he said.

There was something about the voice that made
the Stinkers leap to their feet, throw up their arms
and scream and stamp. It was Mayhem.

22   Chuckle and Gloat

Back at the police-station, Inspector Mayhem couldn't help chuckling to himself and gloating as he surveyed the sorrowful Stinkers.

'Stealing a fire-engine! Bursting a Bouncy Castle! Attempted theft of a model pirate ship! We couldn't let you get away with that.'

'But how did you know where we were hiding?' asked Billy.

'See Chapter 16,' replied the Inspector smugly.

'And how did you know we were going to . . . er . . . borrow the pirate ship?' asked King Pong.

'A little bird told me,' said the Inspector, tapping the side of his nose with a finger, and giving a handful of seeds to the parrot perched on his left shoulder. 'Yes, me and the constables and the firemen enjoyed our little game of pirates this evening, but tomorrow *we* go back to work, while you miserable lot, you go to court.'

'Oh good, will the Queen be there?' asked Sourpuss, all innocence.

'Take 'em away and lock 'em up,' said Mayhem to the Duty Sergeant, and then added, rather meanly, 'and no bedtime story for the cat!'

23 Dry Dock

The Magistrate (whose name I forget) was a fine-looking woman with wild red hair and an eyepatch.

'Stinkers,' she said, addressing them in a stern, magisterial voice, 'you will be upstanding while the court passes sentence.'

The Stinkers did as they were commanded and upstood, feeling very nervous indeed.

The Magistrate looked at each one fiercely and then at the notebook in front of her. Slowly and thoughtfully she picked up a pen and began to scribble.

What is she writing? thought the Stinkers.

24 What is She Writing?

Have a look at the back and find out.

25   The End of It

At last the Magistrate put down her pen, tore a page out of the notebook, folded it and asked the Clerk of the Court to pass it to the policeman on duty at the back.

She turned her fierce half-gaze to the Stinkers.

'Right, you miserable lot, and what shall we do with you? If I'm in a bad mood I could send you to prison and let you rot for the rest of your stinky lives.'

The temperature in the courtroom dropped suddenly as the Stinkers' blood ran cold.

'On the other hand, if I'm in a good mood I could let you off with a caution, or think of something worth while for you to do. Now what sort of mood am I in?'

A clock ticked nervously. Someone in the public gallery coughed. The waiting was nerve-racking. The Stinkers could hardly bear the tension.

Then the Magistrate looked beyond the accused to the back of the courtroom, where a smiling policeman waved a piece of notepaper and gave her the thumbs-up sign.

'Yippee!' yelled the Magistrate and with a smile as broad as a Spanish galleon said to the Stinkers, 'OK, you lot, I won't send you to prison this time, but I want you to say sorry to all those people you have been naughty to.'

She fixed Mrs Wobblebottom with her good eye and added, 'And that includes the little girl in the pretty pink dress.'

'I'll buy her a strawberry and vanilla with chocolate chip and maple syrup,' said Mrs W.B., 'with chopped almonds.'

'That's the spirit,' said the Magistrate. 'And to keep you all out of mischief for a while I want you to glue together all the pieces from the Bouncy Castle. Court will adjourn.'

She rose and banged on the desk. But not with
a hammer. The Stinkers saw for the first time
her left arm, which had at the end of it
not a hand
        but a
            shiny
                brass
                    hook

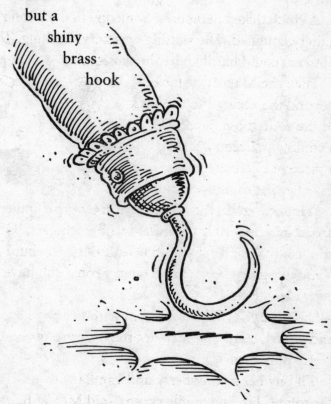

Today in Court

FIRST CASE : Teacher playing truant.
— 6 months jail !

That is a very handsome
policeman standing
at the back......
wonder what his name is ?

Rob ?
Jason ?
Tom ?

Norbert

P.C.
me

Lunch ?
Pizza ?
spag ?
cheese ✓
sandwich

SECOND CASE : The Stinkers!
naughty but not wicked ...... Teach a lesson?
(P.S. They dont half PONG !!!!!)

I fancy seeing that pirate film
tonight — "Cargoes".......

Shall I write a note
P.C. and ask if he
wants to go as well ???